John Burningham
HUSHERBYE

A TOM MASCHLER BOOK
JONATHAN CAPE
London

For Madeleine

Among other books by John Burningham

Borka (Winner of the 1964 Kate Greenaway Award)

Mr Gumpy's Outing (Winner of the 1971 Kate Greenaway Award)

Come Away from the Water, Shirley

Time to Get Out of the Bath, Shirley

Would You Rather...

The Shopping Basket

Avocado Baby

Aldo

Courtney

Granpa (Winner of the 1984 Kurt Maschler Emil Award)

Cloudland

Whadayamean

and the Little Books

The Baby The Blanket The Cupboard The Dog
The Friend The Rabbit The School

First published 2000

1 3 5 7 9 10 8 6 4 2

© John Burningham 2000

John Burningham has asserted his right under the Copyright,
Designs and Patents Act 1988 to be identified as the author of this work. First published in the United
Kingdom 2000 by Jonathan Cape Limited, Random House, 20 Vauxhall Bridge Road, London SW1V 2SA
The Random House Group Limited
Reg No. 954009
A CIP catalogue record of this book
is available from the British Library

0 224 04648 9

Printed in Hong Kong by Midas Printing Ltd.

There's a cat with a pram.
She's had a hard day and
now needs a place for
her kittens to stay.
HUSHERBYE

The baby's been sailing
a boat on the sea,
and now needs to sleep.
HUSHERBYE

There are three tired bears
who are climbing the stairs.
HUSHERBYE

And a fish in the sea,
it is weary you see.
HUSHERBYE

And the man on the moon,
he'll be asleep soon.
HUSHERBYE

The goose flying high
was all day in the sky.
HUSHERBYE

There's a frog who's been hopping all day in the heat, he's tired and he's dry.

HUSHERBYE

Now we are tired,
we need to lie down.
It's time to sleep for the night.

When morning comes
we will wake up again.
Tomorrow will be a new day.

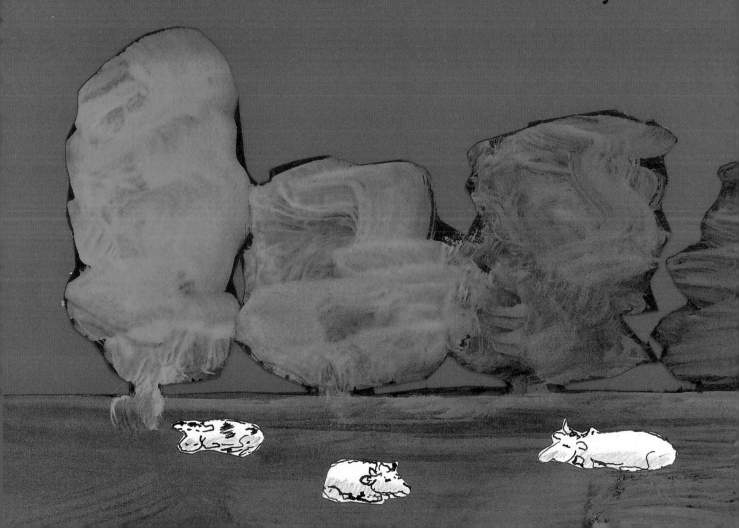

The cat's found a place
for her kittens to stay,
out of the wind and the snow.

The baby's asleep
in the boat that's afloat,
and is rocking on watery waves.

The three tired bears
who were climbing the stairs,
are tucked up in their beds
until morning.

The fish in the deep
has fallen asleep
with his head on a pillow
of coral.

The man in the moon
will not wake until noon.
Then he'll shine up the
moon for tomorrow.

The goose is asleep now,
asleep in the chair,
and will fly off again
when it's light.

The frog did get wet and
now dreams in a net,
and he'll hop off once
more in the morning.

You are tucked up in bed.
Your toes are all warm,
You're out of the wind
and the rain.
Your head's on the pillow
You'll soon be asleep.
HUSHERBYE
HUSHERBYE
HUSH

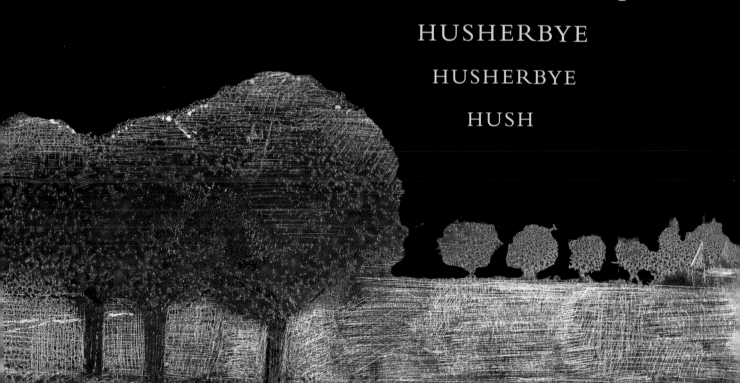